Don't Let the ELEPHANT GO
Modern Nepali Folktales

ATUL POKHAREL

Illustrations by DOINA PARASCHIV

www.mascotbooks.com

Don't Let the Elephant Go: Modern Nepali Folktales

For more information, please contact:
Mascot Books
560 Herndon Parkway #120
Herndon, VA 20170
info@mascotbooks.com

Library of Congress Control Number: 2016908767

CPSIA Code: PBANG0916A
ISBN-13: 978-1-63177-500-0

Printed in the United States

Dedicated to my dear daughter Surabhi.

Don't Let the Elephant Go

One beautiful day, Mira stood on her house's airy veranda. The veranda was on the second story of her house, which was nestled in the southern plain lands of Nepal. It was a small house, constructed of wood and mud, topped off with a roof made of clay tiles.

Mira loved the veranda and she loved to watch the mountains far off in the north. She was only nine years old, but she had spent much of her nine years looking out from the veranda.

Suddenly, Mira heard kids screaming on the front road.

"Elephant! Elephant!" they cried.

There was a big elephant walking on the

road with a man on its back. The elephant was decorated with white and red colored designs on its head and trunk. A group of boys and girls was running around the elephant.

"Stay back!" Mira yelled from the veranda. "Don't get too close! It won't like all the shouting."

The kids did not listen to her.

Mira climbed down from her veranda and went toward the road. She stopped at a safe distance from the elephant and yelled to the kids again, "I can see it clearly from here. Come over here and watch it with me." The kids listened, came over to Mira, and watched the elephant go.

Mira's seven-year-old brother Samir heard Mira's cries and ran out on the veranda. When he saw the elephant, he shouted, "Look, it has two tails!"

The group of kids laughed. "It has only one tail, Samir," said Mira. "The one in the front is its trunk. That's how it eats and drinks water.

That's what's special about elephants."

Then Mira turned to the kids around her and asked, "Do you like elephants?"

"Yes," they all replied.

"They're beautiful animals," said Mira. "I wish I could have one stay in my home with me, but I think they might feel better in the jungle. That's their home."

Mira went back to the veranda. Even after the elephant was gone, she kept thinking about it. She looked at the road and thought that maybe another elephant would walk by. But she didn't see one.

Mira remembered that she had homework to do for school. She went in her room and took out her books and notebooks from her backpack. But she still had the elephant on her mind. She couldn't focus on her homework. She was getting very sleepy.

Suddenly, a small elephant stepped out of her backpack. "Wow!" Mira exclaimed.

The elephant was the size of a toy. It walked

on the table and stopped in front of Mira, greeting her by curling its trunk upward to its forehead. Then it walked all over the room. It walked on the long shelf on the wall, then it jumped from the shelf to the floor and started running wildly.

Mira watched it in disbelief. She had her very own elephant! *Maybe I can take him to school tomorrow and show all my friends,* she thought. Then suddenly the elephant ran toward the door. Mira ran after it, trying to catch the elephant so she could put it back in her backpack. But the elephant was too fast. Mira yelled loudly out her door, "Mommy, don't let the elephant go!"

"What are you talking about, Mira?" Her mother came into her room. "Where's the elephant?"

Mira opened her eyes and realized that it had all been a dream. "Sorry, Mom," she said. "I was dreaming about a toy elephant running around my room. I guess it wasn't real. I'll tell you about it after I finish my homework."

Trick the Trickster

One evening, Mira's mother roasted popcorn in a clay pot. "Do you want some, Mira?" her mother asked.

"Yes, Mommy, thank you," said Mira as she took a handful. "Tonight there will be a full moon. Can I sit on the veranda and watch the moon while I eat?" asked Mira.

"Sure," said Mira's mother, handing her the bowl. "Why do you want to see the moon?"

"Because a full moon is so beautiful and clear. I want to see the craters on it."

Mira carried her popcorn to the veranda. She sat down and looked out for the moon, but she couldn't see it. There was a tree right in the way! So Mira climbed down and went to the yard. There, she saw the moon in the east. *It's still not very clear*, Mira thought. *Those palm leaves are covering half of it.*

Mira was still thinking of where to go to see the moon when her neighbor friend Sarita came over. "Why don't we go to the big field across the road?" she suggested.

"That's a good idea," said Mira. "We can share my popcorn. There aren't any trees to block it there."

So they went to the big field across the road. From there, they saw the moon and its craters much better. White and gray clouds blocked the moon briefly once in a while, but the moon shone bright on the two girls and their bowl of popcorn.

"It looks like the moon's moving fast to escape the clouds," Sarita said.

"No, it's not the moon that's moving, it's the clouds!" said Mira. "The moon's stayed in the same place this whole time, but the clouds haven't."

"Oh, you're right," said Sarita.

"The moon moves around the earth," Mira explained. "It makes one full circle in one month. We see the moon go around the earth overnight, because the earth's spinning."

"That's fascinating," Sarita said as she took another handful of popcorn from the bowl.

Suddenly, Dallu, a ten-year-old boy from the neighborhood, stealthily came up behind the two girls. He was a mischievous boy who wasn't interested in learning new things. He was interested in being a trickster.

Mira saw Dallu out of the corner of her eye. He was trying to grab some popcorn out of her popcorn bowl. He knew Mira saw what he was up to, so he quickly pulled his hand away. "Why are you girls looking at the moon?" he asked instead.

Mira thought of a trick to fool Dallu. "We're looking at the rabbit in the moon," she said.

"A rabbit?" Dallu asked. "Where is it? I can't see it."

"It's there in the moon, just about to jump back to the earth," Mira pointed to the sky.

"I can't see it," Dallu repeated.

"Just walk very slowly a few steps ahead of us and keep silent. You can see it clearly if you walk twenty steps forward and take a long, hard look. I'll walk behind you."

"All right," said Dallu as he started walking slowly.

"Slowly, slowly," said Mira from behind. Her voice was softer and softer and slower and slower, until she stopped saying anything at all.

Dallu stopped far ahead of the girls, still staring into the night sky. "I don't see the rabbit ready to jump back onto the earth. Where is it?"

There was no answer. Dallu looked back. Mira was gone. He looked further back. Sarita was gone too.

Mira and Sarita had tricked the trickster.

Flying Fun

On a clear and bright Saturday, Mira and Samir sat together on the veranda doing their homework. It was a hot day, but a light wind was blowing gently. A bird flew past the veranda.

"Didi, I want to fly like a bird," Samir said as he watched the bird go by.

"Ha-ha, it'd be fun to fly like a bird on such a beautiful day," Mira said. "But you're a human, and humans can't fly like birds."

"They can't fly like birds," Samir said, "but they can fly in other ways, like in airplanes, hang gliders, or hot air balloons."

"It'd be a lot of fun to fly in those," Mira said.

"But we don't have any of those things here," Samir said hanging his head.

"But we still can try to think of something that's just as fun," said Mira. "Let's first finish our homework, and then we'll think of something as fun as a hot air balloon."

"That's a great idea!" said Samir.

Mira and Samir finished their homework, put their backpacks and other things back in their places, then sat down on the veranda to think of a good idea.

"How about something that flies?" Mira suggested. "I know how much you like flying."

"But we'll never be able to have an airplane or a glider here," Samir said.

Mira thought for a while. "Maybe we can make something."

"Like what?" Samir asked.

"What about a paper airplane?"

"I don't like paper airplanes," said Samir.

"Hmm," Mira thought aloud. "We could watch the birds fly."

"I don't want to do that right now."

"How about flying a kite?" Mira suggested.

"Yeah! I love flying kites." Samir was excited.

"Do you know how to make a kite?" asked Mira. "Because I don't."

"I don't either," said Samir sadly. "What should we do?"

Mira saw Daddy in the yard, so she asked him. "Do you know how to make a kite, Daddy?"

"Yes, I do," Daddy said.

"Great!" said Mira and Samir together.

Daddy collected a newspaper, some coconut leaves, rice, and a reel of sewing string. He cut the paper to the right size, put coconut splinters on it and glued them with rice. He knotted the string on the kite perfectly. He even added a long paper tail.

"Wow, this is a beautiful kite," Mira said. Samir nodded his head in agreement.

Then Daddy held the string reel in his hand and Mira threw the kite up in the air. It zoomed upward with the wind.

"AHA!" Mira shouted in excitement.

"AHA!" Samir said and laughed.

"Let's go to the big field across the road," Daddy said. "There's not enough open space here for the kite to fly freely."

So they went to the big field across the road and the kite flew even farther up in the sky. It went up so far, they could barely see it!

Suddenly, the wind became lighter and lighter and the kite dropped down. "Oh, no! The kite's coming down," said Samir nervously.

"Don't worry, we'll find it once it hits the ground," said Mira.

The kite finally dropped completely. It landed on top of some bushes far across the field.

Mira, Samir, and Daddy ran over to the kite. Samir tried to lift the kite up but he couldn't.

"Wait!" Mira said. "The string's tangled up in the grass. Let me see if I can get it out." Mira worked and worked, but she only freed a small piece of the string. The rest was caught in some wild plants nearby.

Samir and Daddy joined Mira's efforts. Even with all three of them working, the string was slow to untangle. Suddenly, the sky started get dark.

"It's going to rain soon," said Mira. "Let's hurry up."

"Let's leave the string and go home before it rains," Samir said. He did not want to get rained on.

"We can't leave the string like this," Mira said, "a bird might get caught in it!"

"You're right," Samir agreed. "I don't want to hurt any birds." He got back to work untangling the string from the bushes. It was almost free!

The sky was still dark overhead, but off in the distance Mira saw a rainbow. "Look!" she said, pointing at it.

"Wow, that's a beautiful rainbow," Samir said. "I love its colors."

"A rainbow means it's raining over there," said Daddy. "Which means it could rain here anytime. Hurry up! Let's go!"

Mira gave the string one last tug and the kite was free! She grabbed it and started to run with Samir and Daddy right next to her.

"I feel a raindrop on my hand!" Samir cried out as he ran.

"I felt one on my forehead!" Mira yelled.

"And I feel one on my ear!" Daddy shouted, shaking his head.

They finally made it home. As they climbed the stairs, the rain grew heavy.

"Was that as fun as a hot air balloon?" Mira asked Samir as they sat on the veranda watching the rain with Daddy.

"It was better than flying in a rocket!" Samir replied with a smile.

Mira, Samir, and Daddy laughed so hard they were almost louder than the rain.

The Most Beautiful Plants Ever

One evening, Mira was helping her mother in the vegetable garden. The flowers and plants looked more beautiful than ever under the sunset and the pink and orange clouds. Mira called her brother. "Come outside and join us, Samir. It's a beautiful evening!"

Samir came outside. "What's so important out here? I was doing my summer break homework."

"We still have lots of time to finish our homework. Let's do something fun! Why don't we plant seeds and grow new plants?" suggested Mira.

"That's a great idea," Samir said. "What shall we plant?"

"I want to plant a pumpkin," said Mira.

"And I want to plant a bean," said Samir.

They asked Mommy for bean and pumpkin seeds. She had a few of each and handed them to Mira and Samir's outstretched arms.

"Aha, we have seeds!" Samir said, clutching the tiny seeds in his hand.

"Let's plant them so they grow every day," said Mira.

They dug a spot in the garden and made some small holes in the soil. Then they put a seed in each hole and covered them with soil.

"Now we need to water them," Samir said. He sprinkled water on them from a watering can.

"Thank you, Samir," Mira said. "We must remember to water them every day. Otherwise they won't grow big!"

"Don't worry, Mira," said Samir. "I'll remember to water them every evening,

The next morning, Mira's grandma came to their home. "I'm here to pick you two up! How would you like to spend some of your summer holiday with me?" she said.

"Aha!" Mira and Samir yelled together. They loved their grandma and were overjoyed to hear why she had come.

Mommy came into the room to see what Mira and Samir were shouting for.

"Mommy, can we really go?" asked Mira.

Mommy nodded and said, "Daddy and I are going to the city. We have some important work to do there. We'll be gone for two weeks, so you two can enjoy that time with Grandma."

"We're staying with Grandma for two weeks?" Mira and Samir said together, smiles spreading across their faces.

"I'll bring my backpack so I can finish my homework there," Mira said.

"Me too," Samir said. "I'm going to pack now!"

That afternoon, they left for Grandma's home. Carrying their backpacks, they walked on gravel roads and trails for an hour before they finally made it.

At Grandma's home they played, ate, and explored everything. That evening, Grandma asked Mira and Samir if they wanted to help her in the garden.

"Sure," said Mira and Samir together. Even though they were tired from their long day, they wanted to help Grandma. They followed her outside to in her beautiful garden.

"Grandma, guess what," Samir said while pulling some weeds. "We planted some beans and pumpkins yesterday."

"That's great, Samir," said Grandma. "I know you two will take good care of them."

"Oh, no!" Samir suddenly exclaimed. "I'm supposed to water the seeds every day. But I can't do that from here. They're not going to grow!"

"You're right," Mira said sadly. "They may sprout a little bit, but with no water, the plants will die in a couple of days."

"Don't worry," said Grandma, "you can plant new seeds here in Grandma's garden."

"But I want to go back home and water my plants," Samir said.

"I wish we could, Samir," said Mira. "But it's a long way back and there's no one at home."

"But Grandma can take us there every evening so we can water the seeds, can't you, Grandma?" Samir asked.

"I wish I could, Samir," said Grandma. "But it's a long way to walk every day. You can plant new seeds here and new seeds when you get back home."

Mira and Samir tried to forget about the seeds they planted back home. They planted new seeds in Grandma's garden: beans, pumpkins, okras, and cucumbers. They watered the seeds every day. A week later, the seeds sprouted into tiny plants with two leaves.

"They're lovely," Mira said.

"I don't want to go back home and leave these plants here," Samir said. "I wish we could take them with us. Or stay here with them."

"Me too," said Mira. "I wish we could stay here forever, but we have to go."

When the two weeks were finally over, Grandma walked Mira and Samir back home. It was a lovely evening and they had their school bags on their backs as they walked back down the gravel roads and trails.

On the way, Grandma told them a story of her own childhood, a story about when she visited her grandma's home. "I planted a banyan tree in their village and it's still there," she said.

"Still there?" Mira was surprised.

"Yes, it's big and old now," Grandma said, "but it's still standing strong."

"Can we go there and see it?" Samir asked.

"Sure, I can take you to that village next year," said Grandma.

When they got home, it was a beautiful night, just like the evening they planted the seeds in their own garden. The sun was setting and the pink and orange clouds once again made the flowers and plants look more beautiful than ever.

Mira and Samir went to the spot where they had planted their seeds. There were newly grown green bean plants and pumpkins!

Mira touched the soil around their plants. It was damp! "Someone has been watering our plants!" she cried.

Samir knelt down next to the plants. "You're right!" Samir shouted with surprise. "There are fresh drops of water on the leaves!"

Suddenly they heard a voice behind them. "Yes, I did that for you, kids." Mira and Samir spun around. It was Aunt Tara, their neighbor!

"I saw you two planting the seeds two weeks ago," she explained. "When you left and there was nobody at home, I couldn't bear to see the tiny little plants dying. So I watered them every evening. Look how beautiful they are now."

"Thank you, Tara Auntie," Mira and Samir said together.

"They are the most beautiful plants ever!" Mira said, smiling down at them.

My Lucky Stone

One Friday evening, Mira was working on her homework on the veranda when her dad joined her.

"Mira, I saw your math teacher yesterday," he said. "She told me you always do your homework and your other teachers said the same thing. They're all very glad you're such a good worker."

"Thank you, Daddy," Mira said.

"No, thank *you*!" Daddy said. "Here, I have a gift for you because you've done so well." Daddy pulled something out of his coat pocket.

"What is it?" Mira said, peeking into Daddy's hands. He handed the thing to her. "It's just a rock, isn't it?"

Daddy laughed. "You're right, Mira. But I have one more real gift for you," he said, as he reached into his pocket again. This time he pulled out a fountain pen.

"Aha, what a nice pen! I like it," said Mira. "It'll remind me to do even better in school. Thank you, Daddy."

"You're welcome," said Daddy. "You can throw away the rock. It was just a joke."

"I might," Mira said, looking at it in her hand. It was a white, smooth rock as big as a cherry. "Actually, I want to keep it."

Samir came from inside and joined them on the veranda. "What type of rock is it?" he asked.

"It's one of the three types of rocks," Mira explained, "igneous, sedimentary, or metamorphic."

"So, which type is this?" asked Samir.

"I don't know. I'll ask my teacher later," Mira replied. "It's my special rock. I'll call it my Lucky Stone."

It soon became dark, so they all headed

inside. Mira finished her homework in her room before going to bed.

The next morning, Mira was opening her backpack on the veranda when she remembered the rock. "Where's my Lucky Stone?" she said aloud.

She looked in her backpack but it wasn't there. She searched the veranda and her room, but still no luck, so she kept looking. She looked under the beds, chairs, and tables all around her house. She searched in the bookshelves and the almirah. She searched every corner of house but did not find it anywhere.

Mira was sad, so she went and found her mom. "Mommy," she said. "I don't want to lose my Lucky Stone. Where could it be? I've looked everywhere!"

"I didn't know you had a lucky stone," Mommy said. "I swept the floor this morning but didn't see anything. But maybe I swept it up and threw it away. I'm sorry, Mira. If I had known you lost your stone, I would have looked for it."

Mira thought for a while and then went to the backyard. *Maybe Mommy flung it here on accident,* she thought.

While Mira was looking for the stone around the cauliflower plants, she heard a bark at the far end of the backyard. It was a little, brown puppy wagging its tail! It looked thin, weak, and hungry, but happy to see Mira. Mira felt sorry for the puppy and patted him on his back and head. This made him wag his tail even more!

"I want to take you home," she said to the puppy.

So Mira took the puppy home and asked her mom, "Mommy, I found a loving puppy in our backyard! Can we keep him?" Mira held up the little, wiggly puppy. "Look, Mommy, he's hungry and helpless, and needs a home. Please, can we keep him?"

"Of course we can," Mommy said.

"Wow!" said Mira. "Thank you, Mommy! I love him!"

Mira's mom gave the puppy something to

eat. Then Mira, Samir, and Mommy bathed him, combed his fur, and made a place for him to rest. After they were done, the puppy was very happy.

Next, Mira and Samir took him into the backyard. They ran around the yard and the puppy ran after them. Then it jumped up on Mira and pulled the end of Mira's pajama shirt pocket. Mira put her hand in the pocket and felt something familiar. "Oh, it's my Lucky Stone!" she yelled.

"It was in your pocket and you didn't even know it?" Samir asked.

"Nope!" said Mira giggling. "But it's a lucky mistake to make." Mira looked at the stone in her hand, then at their new puppy. "We should call him Lucky."

"That's a great name!" said Samir. Then he turned to the new puppy and said "Hi, Lucky! Chase me next! It's my turn to see if there's anything hidden in my pockets!"

Rainbow on the Road

One Saturday morning, Mira and Samir were playing with Lucky in the front yard of their home. The sky was overcast with dark clouds. They saw lightning, and then they heard thunder.

"It is going to rain soon," said Mira. They ran to the house, and Lucky followed them.

No sooner had Mira, Samir, and Lucky reached the veranda than it started raining heavily. They watched the rain and stretched their hands out to feel the raindrops on their palms. The shower made a heavy sound on the clay ties of the roof above, like one hundred small drums being played together.

Lucky also enjoyed the rain. He looked at it

and barked, *Arf, arf, arf! Woof, woof woof! Bow, bow, bow!*

"I feel like playing in the rain," Samir said, "but I don't know what to do."

"You can make a paper boat to float in the puddles after the rain is over," Mira suggested.

"You can pretend that you're Lucky, and write down how you feel about this rain," Samir said.

"These are great ideas!" said Mira. "Let's do them!"

They went inside to get some paper. Their dad was there, repairing a wall clock.

He said, "You can play, but for just one hour, because I need your help with some work." Pointing at the clock, he said, "It is twelve o'clock now. Be sure to come back at one o'clock." He hung the clock on the wall.

"No problem!" Mira said.

In separate corners of the veranda, Mira and Samir worked on their projects. It didn't take them long to finish. By the time they were done, the rain had stopped and everywhere around the house was flooded with rainwater.

"It looks like a pond," Mira said.

The road wasn't covered in water, but a stream of rainwater flowed like a river alongside of it.

"It is the perfect time to sail my boat. Let's go!" Samir shouted.

Samir placed the paper boat on the rainwater in the yard. Lucky joined them and wagged his tail. The boat slowly floated towards the road, until Samir picked it up and placed it in the stream running next to the other side of the road. Mira and Samir ran and followed the boat.

Lucky ran along with them and said, *Arf, arf, arf! Woof, woof, woof! Bow, bow, bow.*

After a while, Mira realized that they had gone too far from home.

"Let's go back," Mira said to Samir.

Samir tried to catch the boat, but the stream was too wide for him to reach it. He was about to go into the water, but Mira warned him, "You don't know how deep and strong the water is. It may not be safe."

Mira looked around to see if she could find someone to help them. The boat kept floating and Mira and Samir kept following it.

Mira saw her neighbor friend Sarita. "Can you help catch the boat, Sarita?" Mira asked.

Sarita tried but she couldn't catch it either. She ran along with Mira and Samir.

A little farther, Mira saw Dallu, the trickster boy who liked to steal stuff that belonged to other people. Mira asked him to help catch the boat. *Maybe I will be able to steal it*, he thought. So he tried to catch the boat, but all his attempts were in vain. He ran along with them.

They ran further. Mira saw a postman cycling down the road. "Can you please help us catch the boat?" she asked. The postman got off his bicycle and ran along with them, trying to catch the boat. But he was also way too far from the boat.

After a minute, they saw a policeman walking

on the road, waving his stick in the air. "Will you please help us get our boat from the water?" Mira asked him. The policeman hooked his stick on his waist and ran with them. His attempts to catch the boat were not successful either.

A light rain started again. Mira stopped and said to the running crew, "Forget the boat. We need to get out of the rain." She pointed to a nearby house and said, "That's my math teacher's home. Let's go there for shelter."

The six people and Lucky climbed on to the veranda and Mira knocked on the door. Her teacher opened it.

"We were trying to catch a paper boat that Samir made, and we chased it this far. Would you please let us stay here until the rain stops?" Mira asked her teacher.

"Why not?" the teacher said. "Let me make tea, and I will call your dad to let him know you're here."

Lucky looked at the rain from the veranda and said, *Arf, arf, arf! Woof, woof, woof! Bow, bow, bow!*

In an hour, Mira's dad arrived on his bicycle. He was carrying a big bag with seven umbrellas on his back. "I went around the neighborhood to collect umbrellas."

Mira carried Lucky and carried a red umbrella. Behind her, Samir carried an orange one. Following him, Dad carried yellow one over his bicycle. Sarita, Dallu, the postman, and the policeman carried green, blue, indigo, and violet umbrellas, respectively.

On their way back, Mira sang,

> "An army of six and a dog
> ran to catch a boat.
> When they could not, they made
> a rainbow on the road."

They were delighted with Mira's song. So they repeated,

> "An army of six and a dog
> ran to catch a boat.
> When they could not, they made
> a rainbow on the road."

Lucky was so happy that he wagged his tail and sang along, *Arf, arf, arf! Woof, woof, woof! Bow, bow, bow!*

"But Mira," said Samir as they headed home, "we're an army of seven and a dog, not six! You counted wrong!"

"No, I didn't," Mira replied. "What does everyone else think?"

"I know why it's seven!" said the policeman. "Because I am a policeman, not an army man!"

"Not quite," giggled Mira.

"I'm not an army man either," Daddy said, "but I am Ali Baba, on my flying carpet!"

"Daddy!" laughed Mira. "That's not right either!"

"Oh, I know!" shouted Samir suddenly. "An army of six and a dog ran to catch a boat because Daddy wasn't a part of our army yet!"

"That's correct," Mira said. "Daddy only joined us afterwards!"

Everyone was still giggling when the postman found his bicycle on the road and went on his way. Next, the policeman left the group, waiving his stick in the air. Sarita and Dallu went to their homes too.

When Mira, Samir, and Dad got home, Dad said, "I told you to show up at one o'clock so you could help me, but you wasted all my time by running after a paper boat. Look at the clock—it's already been more than two hours."

"No, it hasn't," Samir said playfully, pointing at the wall clock. "It's just quarter past twelve."

Samir was right. After Dad repaired the clock, it had stopped again, fifteen minutes after he had hung it on the wall.

"Oh, no! My clock stopped again!" Dad wailed.

Samir said to Mira, "Well, I made a paper boat and sailed it. What about you?"

"I pretended to be Lucky and wrote a lot of things," Mira said. "Here's a page full of my thoughts and feelings about the rain."

Samir looked at the page and shouted, "WHAT!?"

The page read:

Arf, arf, arf!
Woof, woof, woof!
Bow, bow, bow!

Arf, arf, arf!
Woof, woof, woof!
Bow, bow, bow!
Arf, arf, arf!
Woof, woof, woof!
Bow, bow, bow!

Arf, arf, arf!
Woof, woof, woof!
Bow, bow, bow!

Game Rules

One beautiful evening, Mira and Samir were sitting on the veranda and playing a game they made up themselves.

The game was simple. They watched the road in front of their home. Spotting any passersby, vehicles, or pedestrians, would give them points. If they saw someone heading from left to right, Mira would get a point. If someone passed from right to left, that would give Samir a point. They would watch the road for one hour, and the one who got more points would be the winner.

"There comes a bicycle from the right," Samir said with excitement. "I get a point."

Nothing else appeared for a while. Samir

said, "I don't think anyone else is coming. So, I'm the winner."

"Hey, the game isn't over yet! Just wait, I'll get more points," Mira said. "Look! There's a bullock cart coming from the left, so I get a point!" Mira shouted with joy.

Soon there was a fruit seller coming from the left side, and Mira cried out, "I have two points now!"

Then they saw a cow coming from the right side. Samir cried, "Hurray, I got another point!"

"Wait," Mira said. "We didn't think of animals walking on the road. We only considered human beings."

"But we should consider anything that moves on the road," Samir said.

"I guess you're right. We can set rules for animals too. Let's agree that animals count for scoring a point," Mira said.

"There's no doubt they count," Samir said firmly.

For a moment there was a silence, as Mira

and Samir anxiously watched the road.

"Mira and Samir, what are you doing? Come on in," their mom said from the door.

"Wait," Mira said to her mom. "Look there," she said to Samir. There was an interesting scene on the road. A herd of cows walked on the road from left to right. A cowherd was walking behind the cows, urging them to move faster.

"Wow, there are so many," Mira said. "One, two, three, four—"

There were nine cows and a cowherd. "I get ten more points!" Mira was ecstatic.

"Wait a minute!" Samir shouted. Then he said, "I don't think we should count animals."

"Are you serious?" Mira was surprised. "You just said a minute ago that you wanted to include animals."

"Hmm—but that was just an error in my thinking. Animals don't count in this game."

"But there was no mistake in my thinking," Mira said confidently. "Animals *do* count in this game—we made it a rule."

"No, animals don't count," Samir insisted.

"Why?" Mira asked.

"Hmm, I believe animals shouldn't count because—" he thought for a second, "because they don't want to walk it themselves. A person makes them walk it. So, let's only count the man."

For a minute, Mira was silent. She was thinking hard. And then she said finally, "You can't change rules in the middle of a game. But I just want the game to go on, if you agree not to change the rules anymore, we can keep playing."

"I agree." Samir was happy.

"All right," Mira said, "I still get one point for the cowherd, and you lose that point you got from a cow."

"Yes, you get that point, and I lose a point," Samir repeated.

Then Dallu appeared on the road, coming from right to left. He was on his new bicycle, ringing the bell. "I scored one more point," Samir cried out.

Dallu stopped and waved his hand at Mira and Samir. "Come here and look at my new bicycle."

Mira and Samir went to the road. "It's a nice bicycle," they said.

"Guess what?" Dallu said, "I can ride it with just one hand on the handle."

Mira said, "That looks cool, but be sure you don't ride with both your hands off."

"I can do that too," Dallu said gleefully. He folded his arms on his chest and rode away.

"He looks like a circus boy," Samir said.

"That's dangerous," Mira said to Samir. "If you ever have your own bike, be sure to hold the handles, or you may fall down and break your bones."

"I'll remember that," Samir said.

Mira and Samir went back to the veranda and continued the game. A little while later, they saw a big group of boys coming from the right side. "WOW," Samir cried out with joy, "that's a ton of points!"

Samir started to count. There were twenty-three of them. Mira noticed that one of them was Dallu. He looked hurt and sad. One of the boys was carrying him on his shoulders.

"Yahoo! I got twenty-three points," Samir yelled.

"Okay, but what happened to Dallu?" Mira asked. They went to the road and asked the boys what was wrong.

"We were playing soccer in the field near the road. Dallu came by on his new bicycle and rang his bell and showed us how he can ride without holding the handle," they explained. "We all cheered, and he drove his bike faster and faster in circles on the soccer field. Then somebody told him, 'Do that with both your feet off the pedals!'"

"What happened after that?" Mira asked.

"He tried to do it, but he lost his balance and fell off the bike and bumped his head. It looks like he broke his leg too. So, we are taking him to hospital."

"Poor boy fell off the bike and gave me almost two dozen points," Samir said to Mira.

"Wait," Mira said to Samir. And then she asked the boys, "You actually don't want to go to the hospital, right? You would rather play soccer?"

"Yes, we'd rather play soccer. Can you take him to hospital?"

"No, I won't do it," Mira turned to Samir. "You don't get any points from these boys."

"Why not?" Samir cried.

"According to your rule, I didn't get any points for the cows that walked on the road, because they didn't want to walk it, but the cowherd made them. Likewise, these boys don't want to go to the hospital. Dallu's the one who made them cancel their soccer game and go to the hospital instead."

Samir was about to say something, but Mira said quickly, "You agreed not to change the rules of the game anymore."

Samir was speechless.

Where is the Flute Seller?

It was the Friday that Mira and Samir had been looking forward to for a long time. After they got home from school, they hurried to get ready to go to the fair.

The fair was held once a year at the weekly market near their village. It took about half an hour of walking to get there. Mira said to Samir, "Hurry up, or we'll be too late to see everything."

"Let me grab the money Dad gave me this morning and I'll be ready," Samir said. "I want to buy a flute."

"Daddy gave me some money too," Mira said.

Off they went. On the way, they saw a lot of

people going to the fair. They were all talking about what they would see and buy there.

In half an hour, they got to the fair. There were many more people than on other Fridays. There were more stalls to buy things from. There were balloon sellers pumping up colorful balloons, surrounded by kids waiting for their turns to buy one. Children were everywhere, buying plastic animals and trumpets, wooden peg tops, clay piggy banks, and much more. A lot of girls were buying clay grinders.

"I don't see a flute seller anywhere," Samir said.

"Don't worry," Mira said. "We will find one soon."

"I hope we do," Samir said. "Why don't we ride the Ferris wheel now?"

"Let's go," said Mira.

Mira and Samir rode the Ferris wheel. When they were at the top, they could see the villages far away. "I think that tiny roof over there is our home." Samir pointed out a house far away.

But soon the house was out of sight, because they were going up and down so quickly. Samir stretched his body and twisted his head so he could see the house again.

"Be careful. Sit relaxed and look to the front," Mira said to Samir.

"Why?" Samir asked.

"Because a small slip can be dangerous," Mira said.

Then suddenly, Samir cried out with joy, "Flute!"

From the height of the Ferris wheel, they saw a flute seller holding a pole with a big bunch of bamboo flutes of different sizes on it.

"I want the Ferris wheel to stop now, because I want to buy a flute," Samir said.

Mira laughed as she said, "Stop, Ferris wheel, stop! Samir wants to buy a flute."

"You're funny," said Samir.

After a while, the wheel stopped and Samir ran to get to the flute seller.

"Don't run away from me, Samir," Mira

yelled. "You might get lost."

There on the ground, they didn't see the flute seller.

"I saw him somewhere over here, but I can't find him now," said Samir.

"Don't worry, we will find him soon."

Mira and Samir looked for the flute seller everywhere in the crowd. They went to every stall. They went around the Ferris wheel again and again. But the flute seller was nowhere to be seen.

"Oh, I am so unlucky," Samir said sadly.

"Be patient, Samir," Mira said. "We'll find him eventually, and you'll be even happier in the end."

While they were looking for the flute seller, they saw a crowd around a monkey show. They stood and watched the show.

The *madari* was telling his two monkeys to walk, dance, and play. The man made a round loop of rope and the monkeys jumped through it. He asked them to show the crowd how a gentleman walks. The spectators watched and laughed as the monkey strutted around.

"How do monkeys know human language?" Samir asked Mira.

"I bet they don't actually understand what the man says, but he has trained them somehow," Mira explained.

Finally, the *madari* ordered his monkeys to go to the people and collect money for the show. Quickly, one of the monkeys ran to the spectators and stretched out his hand to ask for money. While doing so, the monkey touched a man's legs. The man was so scared that he leaped back and bumped into other people in the crowd and then fell on the ground. He was holding a pole that fell too. From the top of the pole, many flutes dropped and scattered on the ground.

"The flute seller!" Samir exclaimed.

The man rose. Mira and Samir helped him collect his flutes. When they were done, the man said, "Thank you, kids, for your help. I want to give you each a flute."

When Samir tried to give him money, the flute seller said, "This is my gift to you, because I'm grateful that you helped me."

"Oh, we only helped a little," Mira said, "but we want to buy one. Actually, we were looking for you for a long time."

Mira and Samir tried to insist the flute seller take the money, but he would not.

"Okay then," Mira and Samir said. "Thank you very much."

"Thank you," the flute seller said.

Mira and Samir moved on. Mira bought a couple of bracelets and a piggy bank for herself. Samir bought a peg top and a colorful pinwheel for himself. Then they went to a food stall and ate some *samosas* and *gulabjamuns*. Finally, they headed back home with their new treasures.

Red, Flying Eagle

It was the day before the Dashain holidays when Mira and Samir came out of their classrooms at school to find their parents waiting for them.

"We've come to pick you up to go to the bazaar," Mommy said.

"We want to buy your Dashain clothes today," Daddy said.

"YAY!" Samir and Mira yelled with joy.

Outside the school, Daddy unlocked his bicycle and said, "I'll see you at the bazaar." Off he rode, out of sight.

Mommy stopped a rickshaw, and the three of them got on.

It was a beautiful day. There were big green paddy fields on both sides of the road. The rice stems were still green and soft. The beautiful leaves swayed in the light breeze.

Samir said to Mira, "It's nice to go to the bazaar straight from school."

"Yes, it is," Mira said. "But why do we have to hurry? We still have a couple days before Dashain, and we could do the shopping tomorrow."

"I want to do it today because I need to save time," Mommy said. "There are a lot of other things to do to prepare for the festivals."

"Oh, yes," Samir said. "We have a lot of things to do. I'll clean the house, scrub the doors and windows."

"And I'll help Momma cook food," Mira said.

The rickshaw drove past ponds of beautiful water hyacinths. As they passed, the hyacinths' light purple flowers glowed among the shiny green leaves in the water. "These flowers look marvelous," Samir said. "Can we plant them in our backyard garden?"

"They do look awesome," Mira said.

"But *jalkumbhi* is a wild water plant, and we can't plant them in our garden. They grow and spread over a pond so fast that they block sunlight from going into the water, which fish and other animals don't like. They originally came from South America."

"Oh, I see why they're better off in ponds than in our garden," Samir said. "But how did you know all that?" he wondered.

"It was in a magazine article that was used as a grocery wrapper for the stuff Momma brought home last week."

The rickshaw driver was listening to the conversation behind him. He turned his head back to them and said to Mira, "You're a very smart girl."

"Thank you," Mira said.

A little way further, the road was crumbled, and the wheels of the rickshaw could hardly move over the uneven rocks. The driver pressed the pedals hard, with the full weight of his body, but the rickshaw only moved forward a little. "Stop, brother," Mira said to the driver. Then she said to Mommy and Samir, "Let's get off and help him."

Mira, Samir, and Mommy pushed the rickshaw from behind. When they crossed over the bad part of the road, they got on the rickshaw again and rode smoothly on the even road up to the bazaar.

At the bazaar, Daddy saw them walking up a footpath. He stopped his bicycle and locked it at the side of the road. Then they went into a clothing store.

"I want a shirt like this." Samir pointed at the shopkeeper.

"Which one?" The shopkeeper turned to look at the shirts hanging behind him.

"No," Samir said, "the one you are wearing." He pointed at the shirt the shopkeeper had on. "The one with an eagle on it."

The shopkeeper was wearing a yellow shirt that had a picture of a red flying eagle on the left side of the chest. "Sorry, I don't carry this shirt in my store," the shopkeeper said. "I have many other nice shirts, though."

"But I want a shirt with an eagle," Samir insisted. So the family left that store to look for a shirt with an eagle.

At another store, Mira bought a maroon velvet dress. At another, she found a nice pair of sandals with pearls on them. She bought some other stuff, like hairbands and hair clips.

Daddy and Mommy asked Samir to buy shoes and other stuff, but he was so focused on finding a shirt with an eagle that he did not want to think of anything else. They wandered from one shop to another, looking for a shirt with an eagle, but they didn't find one.

After an hour, Daddy looked at his watch and said, "It's getting late. Either you buy a nice shirt with no eagle on it, and also get your other stuff quickly, or you've wasted all your time, and go home with nothing." He drew his watch closer to his eyes and said, "You have one minute to decide, and the time starts now."

Samir waited about half a minute and then said sadly, "I want to go ahead and buy a nice shirt without an eagle."

Samir bought a pair of shoes, cloth to make pants, and a nice yellow shirt.

Mommy and Daddy bought clothes and other stuff for themselves, and then they went to a tailor.

At the tailor's workshop, a group of men were busy sewing clothes. Samir was amused at how fast the men were pedaling the sewing machines. The master tailor drew Samir over and started taking measurements for his pants. After he finished writing down the measurements, he stretched his measuring tape over Samir's shoulder.

"I'm not having a shirt made here," Samir said. "I have a ready-made one."

"Oh, okay," the tailor said. "It must be a nice one."

"Yes, it is. But I wish it had an eagle on it," said Samir. "We searched for one for a long time, but we didn't find any."

"I can help you with that," the tailor said. "Would you like an eagle patched on your shirt?"

"Sure," Samir's face brightened. "Do you have a red one?"

"Let me see," the tailor said, opening a drawer. He took out a red flying eagle. "How's this?"

"That's perfect," Samir smiled. "Thank you, brother."

"You're welcome! It'll be ready on Monday," the shopkeeper said.

Samir couldn't wait.

Dashain and Tihar

It was the season of Dashain, the greatest festival in Nepal. Mira woke up before sunrise and went to the veranda where her mother was sweeping the yard. To the side of the house, there was a *parijat* shrub as tall as the veranda loaded with blooming tiny white flowers. Mira smelled their fragrance in the air. She took a basket and went down to the front yard.

"Why did you wake up so early?" Mommy asked.

"I want to collect some of these nice smelling flowers," Mira said. She went to the plant and picked the flowers that had fallen off the shrub onto the ground below it. They were cool and soaked by dew. By the time her basket was full, the sky was bright with the sunrise.

Mira saw Samir in the front yard. "Why did you wake up so early?" Mira asked.

"I want to go and play on the *lingey ping*."

Mira and Samir went to the big field across the road in front of their home. There was a huge swing hanging from the top of four bamboo poles. It was as tall as the top of their house. Samir sat on the swing and Mira pushed him from behind. When Samir had played for a while, it was Mira's turn to sit, and Samir pushed her. Soon, a bunch of other kids came and waited for their turn to play on the swing. After about an hour, Mommy waved at them from the veranda and asked them to come home. They went home, and saw from the veranda that a lot of boys, girls, men, and women were waiting at the swing for their turn and cheering every time someone was swinging way up in the air.

"We were smart to wake up early in the morning and play on the swing, weren't we?"

Samir said to Mira.

"Yes, we were," Mira said. "Tika day will be even more fun."

The most important day of the festival, Vijaya Dashami, finally arrived. Mira and Samir woke up early in the morning, bathed, and put on their new clothes. They helped their mom and dad arrange and decorate the room to apply tika. They laid down a nice colorful carpet and put flowers in vases. They mixed raw rice, red *abir* dye, and some yogurt, getting the tika ready to apply at the most auspicious time. The radio said that the starting time was ten in the morning that year.

When it was ten o'clock, Daddy put red tika on Mommy's forehead, and said many blessings. Then he put some *jamara* on Mommy's head. She clipped those pale green barley stems in her hair. They were soft plants about four inches long, grown in a dark room just for this festival.

"You look pretty," Mira said to her mom.

Then Daddy and Mommy put tika on Mira's forehead together. "May you be a nice, beautiful, educated, and rich person when you grow up," Daddy said.

"May you be a very kind person and have the means and heart to help needy people," Mommy said.

They showered Mira with blessings.

Then it was Samir's turn. The family looked beautiful with red tika on their foreheads, *jamara* on their heads, and new clothes.

Soon, relatives started arriving. Daddy and Mommy were busy putting tika on them. It was a lot of fun eating, talking, and laughing afterwards. When they were done at their house, the family went to their relatives' homes. The day was so merry and busy that it passed quickly.

When Dashain was over, Samir felt sad. "I want every day to be like Dashain," he said.

"It can't be, Samir," Mira said. "But the second biggest festival, Tihar, is coming in just a month."

"Oh, yes! I like all the lighting and *deusi-bhailo* singing," Samir exclaimed with joy. "I like Tihar even more than I like Dashain."

The first day of Tihar was dedicated to crows. Before they had their lunch, Mira put some food on a leaf plate and put it in the front yard. A crow flew over and started eating it. Mira was overjoyed.

"How was it that you left the food for the crows, and a crow really ate it?" Samir asked her. "It could have been eaten by a dog or any other bird, couldn't it?"

"It doesn't happen all the time," Mira said, "but I'm happy that it did this year."

The next day was dedicated to dogs. Mira prepared a special meal of rice and milk for Lucky, and they put a flowery garland around his neck. They put some tika on Lucky's forehead. He looked very happy, and wagged his tail as he ate his special food.

On the morning of the third day, the family worshipped a cow. Daddy and Mommy put a marigold garland around the cow's neck and put colors on her forehead and body. Daddy turned to Mira and Samir and asked, "Kids, do you know why we worship a cow?"

"I know!" said Samir. "Because a cow is a cool animal!"

Mira laughed. "That's true Samir, but it's because a cow is another form of the goddess of wealth, Laxmi."

"And this is what's special about today, Laxmipooja," finished Daddy.

The third day was dedicated to the goddess of wealth. The family cleaned the road in front of the house and decorated the veranda to welcome the goddess into their home. When it got dark that evening, they lit candles and clay lights all over the veranda rails. They even lit candles at the entrance to the front yard. The house looked so pretty that Samir started jumping and yelling, "Today's the best day of the year!"

A group of neighbor girls came, singing

Bhailo. They wore traditional clothes, and they even sang some other songs and danced. Mommy gave them some money and some homemade delicacies, special for Tihar. Mira wore her traditional dress, *gunyu choli*, and went with the girls to other homes, singing Bhailo.

The next day was dedicated to oxen and farming. The house was bright with lights, like the previous day. It was the boys' day to go around the neighborhood, singing Deusi. Samir wore a *dhaka topi* and sang and danced with his friends. At the end of Deusi, he came home happy, with money in his pocket. "We collected forty-eight rupees each," he said with pride.

The final day, Bhaitika, was the most special day for Mira and Samir. At about ten in the morning, Mira put tika on Samir's forehead. It was the day of tika for brothers.

The tika was different from the one at Dashain. Mira painted tiny dots of seven colors that made a long, slim, colorful, vertical tika on Samir's forehead. Then she put a garland made of *makhmali* flowers on him. She gave him *selroti*, sweets, and other delicacies. In turn, Samir put tika on Mira's forehead and gave her some money in an envelope. Mommy helped them, but then quickly ran to the kitchen.

"Mommy, when did people start celebrating Bhaitika?" Samir asked her.

"I'm busy," Mommy yelled from the kitchen. "My brothers are arriving soon to receive tika from me. I can't explain it to you right now, it's too hectic."

"Oh, maybe I can ask Daddy. Where is he?" Samir asked Mira.

"Daddy has just left for his sister's home to receive tika," said Mira.

"Oh," said Samir. "Do you know the answer to my question?"

"I just know that we have been celebrating Bhaitika for a long time."

"So, when we grow up, will you still put tika on me, like Mommy and Daddy are doing with their brothers and sisters?" Samir asked Mira.

"I hope we'll do this every year," Mira said.

"But it'll depend on how far you live from me."

"I will always come to you to receive tika, even if I live seven seas away from you, Mira," Samir said, with tears in his eyes.

"Oh, I love you, Samir," Mira said, with tears in her eyes too.

"I love you, Mira, dearest sister in the whole wide world."

About the Author

Atul Pokharel lives in Kentucky with his wife and two daughters. He grew up in Biratnagar, Nepal and spent most of his twenties in Kathmandu, before moving to America in 2007. Pokharel brings you a lot of fun, zest, and laughter from the curious world of Nepal.

Have a book idea?
Contact us at:

info@mascotbooks.com | www.mascotbooks.com